C0-BWW-955

Curly's MOJO® amazing stuff™

ALL THE FOOD I DIDN`T EAT WHILE COLORING

CONFESSIONS, RECIPES AND REGRETS FROM A COLORING ADDICT

ILLUSTRATIONS BY

HOWARD "CURLY" GREENBERG

TEXT & DESIGN BY "MO" JOE SHANSKY

(CHILDHOOD BUDDIES FROM BROOKLYN)

PRINTED IN THE U.S.A.

PUBLISHED BY CURLY`S MOJO®
5 HANLEY FARM ROAD, WARREN, RHODE ISLAND 02885
DISTRIBUTED BY CURLYSMOJO.COM

Sturgeon General's WARNING THIS COLORING BOOK OF RECIPES IS NOT A DIET COOKBOOK, NOR PART OF ANY RECOGNIZED 12 STEP PROGRAM. IT IS THE RAMBLINGS OF AN ARTIST AND HIS CERTIFIABLE CHILDHOOD BUDDY FROM BROOKLYN. HOWEVER, LAUGHING IS CONTAGEOUS.

With this pizza, it's sink or swim

Hello Everyone. My name is Curly and I am a coloring addict. (Hello Curly)

As a coloring addict I missed supper with my family many times. Coloring to me was all consuming (pardon the pun). What I missed most of all was pizza night with the kids. My wife made a wonderful pizza on Wednesdays. It had everything on it... three cheeses, peppers, sausages, pepperoni, onions, ham, you name it! But most of all I missed sharing the family's daily adventures, watching the kids grow up, learning who their friends were and lots of other family-oriented activities... All because I was coloring. Here is the recipe for my wife's pizza. Enjoy a slice for me, won't you?

The Kitchen -Sink Pizza Recipe

INGREDIENTS:

Olive oil
Cornmeal (to help slide the pizza onto the baking sheet)

Tomato sauce (smooth, or puréed)
Mozzarella cheese, grated
Parmesan cheese, grated
Feta cheese, crumbled
Mushrooms, thinly sliced
Bell peppers, stems and seeds removed, thinly sliced
Italian sausage, cooked ahead and crumbled
Chopped fresh basil
Pesto
Pepperoni, thinly sliced
Onions, thinly sliced
Ham, thinly sliced

Prep time: 1 hour
Cook time: 30 minutes
Yield: Makes One 10-12-inch pizza.

Pre-made Pizza dough is a yeasted dough which can be purchased in supermarkets or Italian bakeries in the frozen section.

PREPARATION:

1- Place a pizza stone on a rack in the lower third of your oven. Preheat the oven to 450°F for at least 30 minutes, preferably an hour.

2- Remove the plastic cover from the dough and punch the dough down so it deflates a bit. Divide the dough in half. Form two round balls of dough. Place each in its own bowl, cover with plastic and let sit for 10 minutes.

3- Prepare your desired toppings. Note that you are not going to want to load up each pizza with a lot of toppings as the crust will end up not crisp that way. About a third a cup each of tomato sauce and cheese would be sufficient for one pizza. One to two mushrooms thinly sliced will cover a pizza.

4- Take the ball of dough and flatten it with your hands on a slightly floured work surface. Starting at the center and working outwards, use your fingertips to press the dough to 1/2-inch thick. Turn and stretch the dough until it will not stretch further. Let the dough relax 5 minutes and then continue to stretch it until it reaches the desired diameter - 10 to 12 inches. Use your palm to flatten the edge of the dough where it is thicker. You can pinch the very edges if you want to form a lip.

5- Brush the top of the dough with olive oil (to prevent it from getting soggy from the toppings). Use your finger tips to press down and make dents along the surface of the dough to prevent bubbling. Let rest another 5 minutes.

6- Lightly sprinkle your pizza baking sheet with corn meal. Transfer one prepared flattened dough to the pizza sheet. If the dough has lost its shape in the transfer, lightly shape it to the desired dimensions.

7- Spoon on the tomato sauce, sprinkle with cheese, and place your chosen toppings on the pizza.

8- Bake pizza until the crust is browned and the cheese is golden, about 10-15 minutes. If you want, toward the end of the cooking time you can sprinkle on a little more cheese.

Recipe modified from Simply Recipes by Elise Bauer

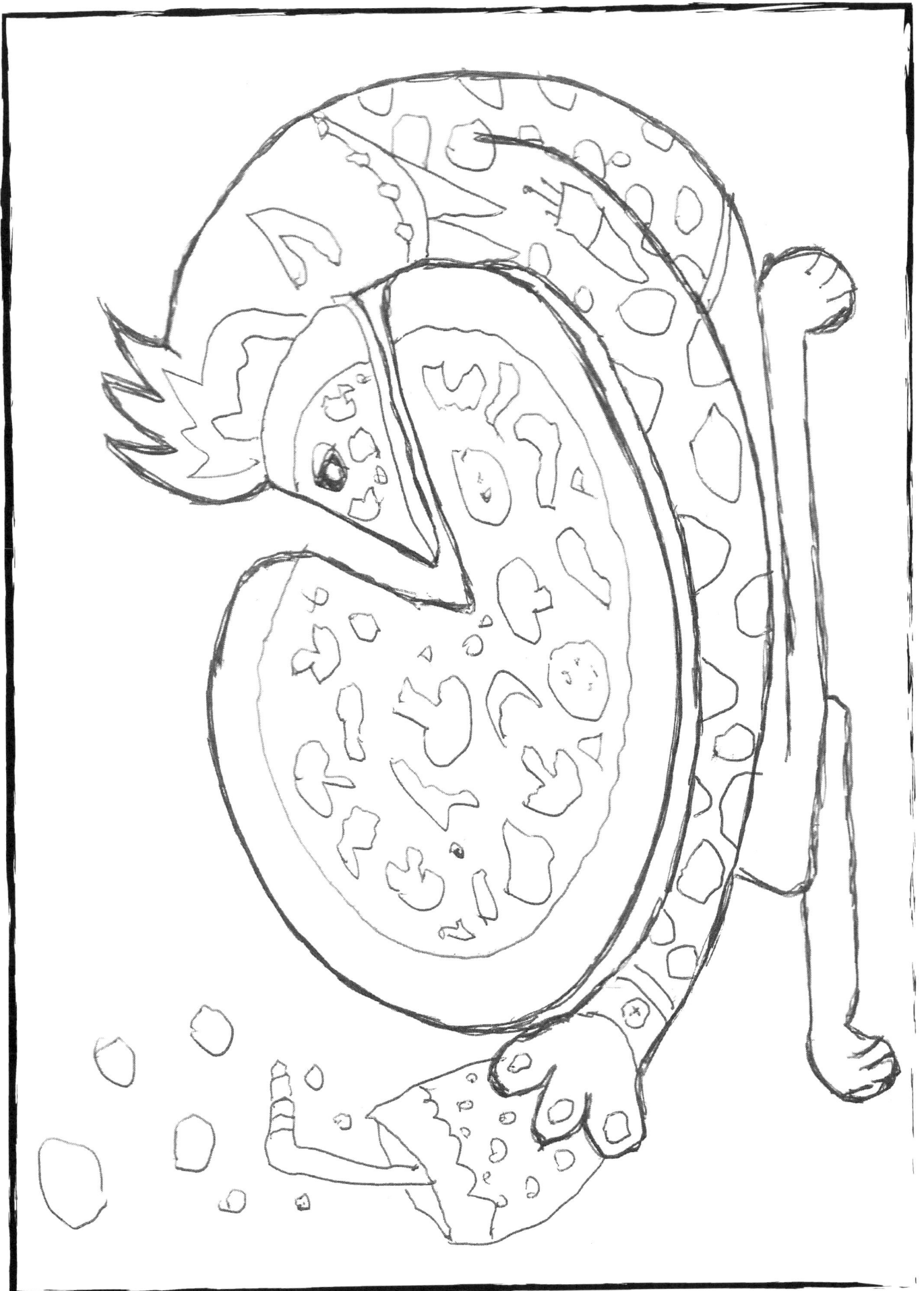

Honolulu Luau Turkey Burgers

Hello Everyone. My name is Curly and I am a coloring addict. (Hello Curly)

I could have been present for this mouth-watering, appetite-devouring morsel... but I wasn't. I was upstairs, watching my 19" black and white TV and coloring a picture of a flower while my family was treated to a sumptuous dinner next door. My next door neighbor made an incredible feast and my family enjoyed it without me. I just can't eat when I'm coloring... I can't concentrate on what I'm coloring and eat at the same time. And right now the coloring trumps any juicy, delicious, tempting or social distraction hands down.

So here's Larry's recipe for the Honolulu Luau Burgers. Serves four people. Follow it carefully and savor one for me while I suffer and try to inhale the aroma wafting from my neighbor's kitchen. Thanks.

INGREDIENTS:
Honolulu Luau Turkey Burger:

1 can (8 ounces) sliced pineapple
1/2 cup dry bread crumbs
1/2 cup sliced green onions
1/2 cup chopped sweet red pepper
1 tablespoon reduced-sodium soy sauce
1/4 teaspoon salt
1 pound lean ground turkey
1/4 cup reduced-sodium teriyaki sauce
4 sesame hamburger buns

TOPPINGS:
8 slices Applewood smoked bacon
4 fresh pineapple slices, 1/2-inch thick
1/4 cup unsalted butter, melted
1/4 cup brown sugar
4 slices mozzarella cheese

Boston lettuce
2 ripe tomatoes, sliced into rounds
8 pickle slices

OPTIONAL:
1/3 cup prepared mayonnaise
2 chipotle peppers in adobo sauce

DIRECTIONS:

Drain pineapple, reserving 1/4 cup juice (discard remaining juice or save for another use); set pineapple aside. In a large bowl, combine the bread crumbs, onions, red pepper, soy sauce, salt and reserved pineapple juice. Crumble turkey over mixture and mix well. Shape into four patties.

Using long-handled tongs, moisten a paper towel with cooking oil and lightly coat the grill rack. Grill, covered, over medium heat for 3 minutes on each side. Brush with teriyaki sauce. Grill 4-6 minutes longer on each side or until a meat thermometer reads 165° and juices run clear.

Grill pineapple slices for 2 minutes on each side, basting occasionally with teriyaki sauce. Warm buns on grill; top each with a burger and pineapple slice. Yield: 4 servings.

Modified from original recipe on The Taste of Home website by Babette Watterson

Fishy-soir

Hello Everyone. My name is Curly and I am a coloring addict. (Hello Curly)

My sister, Linda, makes a claypot fish and potatoes to die for. This culinary critique is from my family and my brother-in-law Alan who actually gets to sample it while I'm coloring some aquatic scene in their den while they are dining and laughing at my self-imposed predicament. I know what I'm missing. Coloring is my "Moby Dick" (to stretch a metaphor) and the crayon is my harpoon. You would think that the wonderful smells emanating from my sister's kitchen would over-ride my compulsion to color... but no, I am not drawn to the dining table where gastronomic delights sing a siren song to my waiting tastebuds. So, here is Linda's recipe. It will make me feel better knowing that you will appreciate this gourmet dish.

Claypot Fish and Potatoes

INGREDIENTS:

3 Yukon potatoes, sliced into 1/4-inch slices
Salt and freshly ground pepper
1/4 cup olive oil, plus extra for greasing dish and brushing on lemons
3/4 pound white fish fillets, such as cod, flounder or tilapia
4 cloves garlic, minced
2 teaspoons minced fresh thyme
1/2 lemon, juiced
1 yellow onion, sliced
3 Roma tomatoes, thickly sliced
1/2 cup good quality black olives, pitted and lightly crushed and sliced in half
1 lemon, quartered
Special Equipment: 15 1/2-by-7 1/2-inch terracotta cazuela (baking dish)

DIRECTIONS:

Preheat the oven to 375 degrees F.

Boil the potato slices in salted water until they are not quite completely cooked, about 5 minutes. Drain and set aside. Grease a claypot or baking dish with the olive oil and place the fish in the dish.

In a medium bowl, whisk together the 1/4 cup olive oil, garlic, thyme, lemon, salt, and pepper. Add the onion, tomatoes, olives, and potatoes. Toss gently to coat.

Pour the vinaigrette and vegetables over the fish. Bake in oven until fish is cooked through, about 15 minutes. Meanwhile, brush the exposed lemon quarters with a little olive oil, and in a small grill pan, grill the quartered lemon sections just to give a hint of charred color. Serve the fish with grilled lemon wedges.

Recipe originally found on The Food Network courtesy of Melissa d'Arabian

Just Desserts? Ha!

Hello Everyone. My name is Curly and I am a coloring addict. (Hello Curly)

Well as Frank Sinatra used to sing in the song, "*My Way*,…
Regrets, I've had a few;
But then again, too few to mention.
I did what I had to do
And saw it through without exemption…"
This is one of those few times I regret not putting the crayon down and joining the family enjoying "*the most delicious cupcake in the world*." I don't handout acolades lightly but these cupcakes deserve the title and more. You try out the recipe and see if you don't do what Wayne and Garth do on *Wayne's World*…(I'm not worthy, I'm not worthy)

Chocolate Bourbon Pecan Pie Cupcakes With Butter Pecan Frosting
Cook time: 30 minutes, Total time: 2 hours, Yields: 18 cupcakes

INGREDIENTS:

Bourbon Chocolate Cupcakes
1 cup bourbon*
1 cup canola oil
3/4 cup unsweetened cocoa powder
2 cups all-purpose flour
1 1/4 cups sugar
3/4 teaspoon salt
1 1/2 teaspoons baking soda
2 large eggs
2/3 cup greek yogurt

Pecan Pie Filling
2 tablespoons cornstarch
1/4 cup cold water
1/2 cup brown sugar
3/4 cup corn syrup
3 eggs
1/4 teaspoon salt
1 cup chopped pecans
2 tablespoons bourbon
1 teaspoon vanilla extract

Butter Pecan Frosting:
1/4 cup (1/2 stick) butter
2/3 cup heavy cream
1 cup + 2 tablespoons packed brown sugar
1/2 cup (1 stick) butter, softened
3 cups powdered sugar
1 tablespoon + 1 teaspoon vanilla extract, divided
2 tablespoons bourbon
1/4 teaspoon cinnamon
1 1/2 cup finely chopped raw pecans + 18 whole pecans

INSTRUCTIONS:

Preheat oven to 350 degrees F. Line 2 standard cupcake pans with 18 liners.
In a medium bowl whisk together the bourbon, canola oil and cocoa powder until smooth and creamy.
In a separate bowl, beat the eggs and greek yogurt with an electric mixer. Slowly add bourbon and cocoa mixture. Combine on medium speed until silky and smooth. Beat in the sugar.

Slowly add flour, salt and baking soda, combining on low speed until just incorporated.

Fill baking cups three-fourths full. Bake for about 18-22 minutes. Allow to cool completely before filling, at least 2 hours or covered overnight.

Meanwhile make the pecan pie filling. Combine 1/4 cup cold water with 2 tablespoons cornstarch, whisk until smooth. Add the brown sugar, corn syrup, eggs, salt and corn starch mixture to a sauce pot. Bring the mixture to a boil, whisking consistently for about 5 minutes. Do not stop whisking the mixture, especially in the beginning or you will end up with scrambled eggs. Remove the mixture from the heat and stir in the pecans, bourbon and vanilla. Allow the mixture to cool a few minutes and then transfer to the fridge for at least one hour or until completely cooled and thickened.

Preheat oven to 350 degrees F. Line a baking sheet with foil or a silicone baking mat.

In a medium sauce pan, melt together 1/4 cup butter, cream, and brown sugar. Bring to a boil and boil for one minute. Remove from the heat and add to the bowl of a stand mixer. Place the bowl in the freezer (or fridge for longer) for 15-20 minutes or until cool.

In a bowl whisk together the bourbon, 1 tablespoon vanilla, 2 tablespoons brown sugar and cinnamon. Add pecans and stir to coat evenly. Transfer nuts to prepared baking pan. Bake for 15 to 20 minutes, stirring occasionally, until toasted. Remove and toss the pecans with 1 tablespoon butter. Allow to cool 10 minutes, set aside.

Now grab the cooled butter mixture and add the remaining 1/2 cup room temperature butter, vanilla and powdered sugar to the bowl and beat together until well combined. Mix in about 1/2 cup of the chopped pecans. If the frosting is not stiff enough to frost the cupcakes place it in the fridge for 30 20-30 minutes or the freezer for 5-15 minutes. The remove and whip it for a few second to get everything smooth again.

To assemble the cupcakes: Use a small paring knife to cut a cone-shaped piece from the center of each cupcake. Fill the hole with the cooled pecan pie filling. Add the frosting (if you want to pipe the frosting on use a circular tip, double the frosting recipe and swirl the frosting on in a circular motion) and sprinkle each cupcake with the remaining pecans. If desired top with 1 whole pecan.

Recipe found on the Huffington Post from Half Baked Harvest

Mojo Marinade? Who woulda thunk?

Hello Everyone. My name is Curly and I am a coloring addict. (Hello Curly)

We were visiting one of our friends one hot summer night and they had prepared one of the most elaborate meals which didn't take any time at all (or so I was told.) Again, I missed out on all the eats because I was I was occupied coloring an intricate picture which needed my full attention . . . my loss, believe me. They had made a Cuban Mojo Marinade for chicken drumsticks and thighs, in other words, the dark meat. I didn't hear the end of it from my wife and kids. So here is the recipe for Cuban Mojo Marinade.

You can use mojo sauce on lots of different foods; like Turkey, Chicken, boiled yucca, grilled seafood and meats, fried green plantain chips (tostones) and more. The authentic mojo is made with juice from sour oranges. It still has that little orangey taste, but its very acid and tart. You can come pretty close by mixing equal amounts of freshly squeezed orange juice with lime juice.

This recipe makes one cup.

Cuban Mojo Marinade Prep Time: 5 minutes – Cook Time: 20 minutes – Total Time: 25 minutes

INGREDIENTS:

1/3 cup olive oil
6 to 8 cloves garlic, thinly sliced or minced
2/3 cup sour orange juice* or lime juice
(or equal portions orange juice and lime juice)
1/2 tsp ground cumin
Salt and freshly ground black pepper, to taste

PREPARATION:

Heat the olive oil in a deep saucepan over medium heat. Add the garlic and cook until fragrant and lightly toasted. Don't let it brown or it will be acrid tasting, just about 30 seconds should do it.

Add the sour orange juice, cumin and salt and pepper. STAND BACK; the sauce may sputter. Bring to a rolling boil. Taste and correct seasoning, if needed

Cool before serving. Mojo is best when served within a couple of hours of making, but it will keep for several days, well capped in a jar or bottle, in the refrigerator.

Cuban Mojo Sauce recipe - courtesy of the Cocina Cubana Club, founded by Pascual Perez & Sonia Martinez

I'm in a pickle, now!

Hello Everyone. My name is Curly and I am a coloring addict. (Hello Curly)

When I was growing up with my best friend Mo, we used to stop by the local food mart on the corner of East 21st Street and Avenue X in Sheepshead Bay for a fresh pickle out of a barrel. It only cost a nickel and boy was it sour. A real "wincer." The store is long gone now but the taste of that pickle lingers on... to this day.

So, I was telling Mo's wife about it and she said she had a recipe for Cucumber Salad, handed down from her mother, great grandma Ethel.

So I said I'd love to taste that Cucumber Salad. And she said she'd make some if I would buy the cucumbers. No Problemo, right? The next time I'm in the market I'll pick some up. Well, it's been years since that offer was made and I still haven't tasted that cucumber salad. It's amazing that my reputation with her hasn't soured!

Great grandma Ethel's cucumber salad recipe.

INGREDIENTS:

2 large cucumbers, scored and sliced thin
1/2 medium onion, sliced thin
1/2 c. white vinegar
1/2 c. sugar
1/2 t. salt

PREPARATION:

Heat vinegar with sugar and salt till they dissolve.
Pour over cukes and onions
Refridgerate 1 day or more, stirring a couple of times/day

Who cut the cheese?

Hello Everyone. My name is Curly and I am a coloring addict. (Hello Curly)

This is what happens when you think outside of the box. My two girls invited 4 friends over one weekend, to do what ever teen-age girls do when they get together; talk about boys, or talk about boys, or possibly talk about boys. So, being the magnanimous father that I am, I volunteered to make them some mac & cheese to munch on while they were possibly discussing boys (Oh DAAAAAD!). Not realizing that there was a box of Kraft in the cabinet and feeling in a creative mood, I started to create this culinary masterpiece that I remembered seeing on the Today show once while I was drawing my ubiquitous doodles. I never got to eat any of this. The doodle was calling me away..

The Ultimate Macaroni and Cheese
Total Time– 1hr 15mins Prep 15 mins, Cook 1 hr. Serves 6-8

INGREDIENTS:

2 lbs elbow macaroni
12 eggs
1 cup cubed Velveeta cheese
1 cup butter, melted
6 cups half-and-half
4 cups grated sharp cheddar cheese
2 cups grated extra sharp white cheddar cheese
1-1/2 cups grated mozzarella cheese
1 cup grated asiago cheese
1 cup grated gruyere cheese
1 cup grated monterey jack cheese
1 cup grated muenster cheese
1/8 teaspoon salt
1 tablespoon black pepper

PREPARATION:

Preheat the oven to 325ºF.

Bring a large saucepan of salted water to a boil. Add the macaroni and cook until slightly al dente, about 10 minutes.

Drain and set aside to keep warm.

Whisk the eggs in a large bowl until frothy.

Combine the eggs with the Velveeta, butter, and 2 cups of the half-and-half in a large bowl.

Add the warm macaroni, tossing until the cheese has melted and the mixture is smooth.

Add the remaining half-and-half, 3 cups of the sharp yellow cheddar (reserve 1 cup), the remaining grated cheeses, and salt and pepper.

Toss until completely combined.

Pour the mixture into a 9 x 13 casserole or baking dish and bake for 30 minutes.

Sprinkle top with the remaining 1 cup of yellow cheddar cheese and bake an additional 30 minutes until golden brown on top.

Serve hot.

As seen on the Today show It has EIGHT types of cheese! It makes a huge casserole, and is a big hit at family gatherings.

Hor's d'oeuvres? These go beyond crackers and cheese

Hello Everyone. My name is Curly and I am a coloring addict. (Hello Curly)

You might not think a spoonful of chives and sriracha sauce would make your eyes close in ecstacy. You would be wrong. You might not think that stuffing some wonton wrappers with the afore-mentioned "doctored" cream cheese would be mind-blowing. Again, you would be mistaken. You might think twice about dropping those wonton purses into some hot cooking oil and frying them up til they are golden brown. And crispy.
But don't think twice... These hor's d'oeuvres are da bomb!

Unfortunately, I can't speak from actual experience because I never actually tasted them... because: 1 - I was coloring in the den, multi-tasking while watching a Ravens game... and 2 - they were all gone by the time I heard all the "ooohs and OMG's and other gastronomic exclamations" from all my inlaws assembled on our patio for a family get-together. Oh well, serves me right... right?

Sriracha and Cream Cheese Wonton Bombs
Prep time: 25 minutes, Total time: 35 minutes, Makes: 16 servings - Feeds between 4 and 16 people depending...

INGREDIENTS:

PREPARATION:

1/2 block (4 ounces) cream cheese, softened

In a large bowl, mix the cream cheese, chives and sriracha sauce.

1 tablespoon chives, finely sliced

Arrange the wonton wrappers on a flat surface. Dollop about a teaspoon of the cream cheese mixture in the center of each wrapper. Dip your finger in a little water and run along the edges of the wrappers. Pull the edges together and twist to seal. Continue until all the wontons are filled and sealed.

1 tablespoon sriracha sauce

16 wonton wrappers

Bring the oil to high heat. In batches, fry the wonton bombs until golden brown and crispy, about two minutes per batch (or less). Continue until all the wonton bombs are fried. Place them on paper towels to drain.

Sweet and sour or sriracha sauce, for dipping

Serve immediately with dipping sauce.

Hot oil, for frying

As seen on Tablespoon.com. Recipe prepared by Bev Cooks

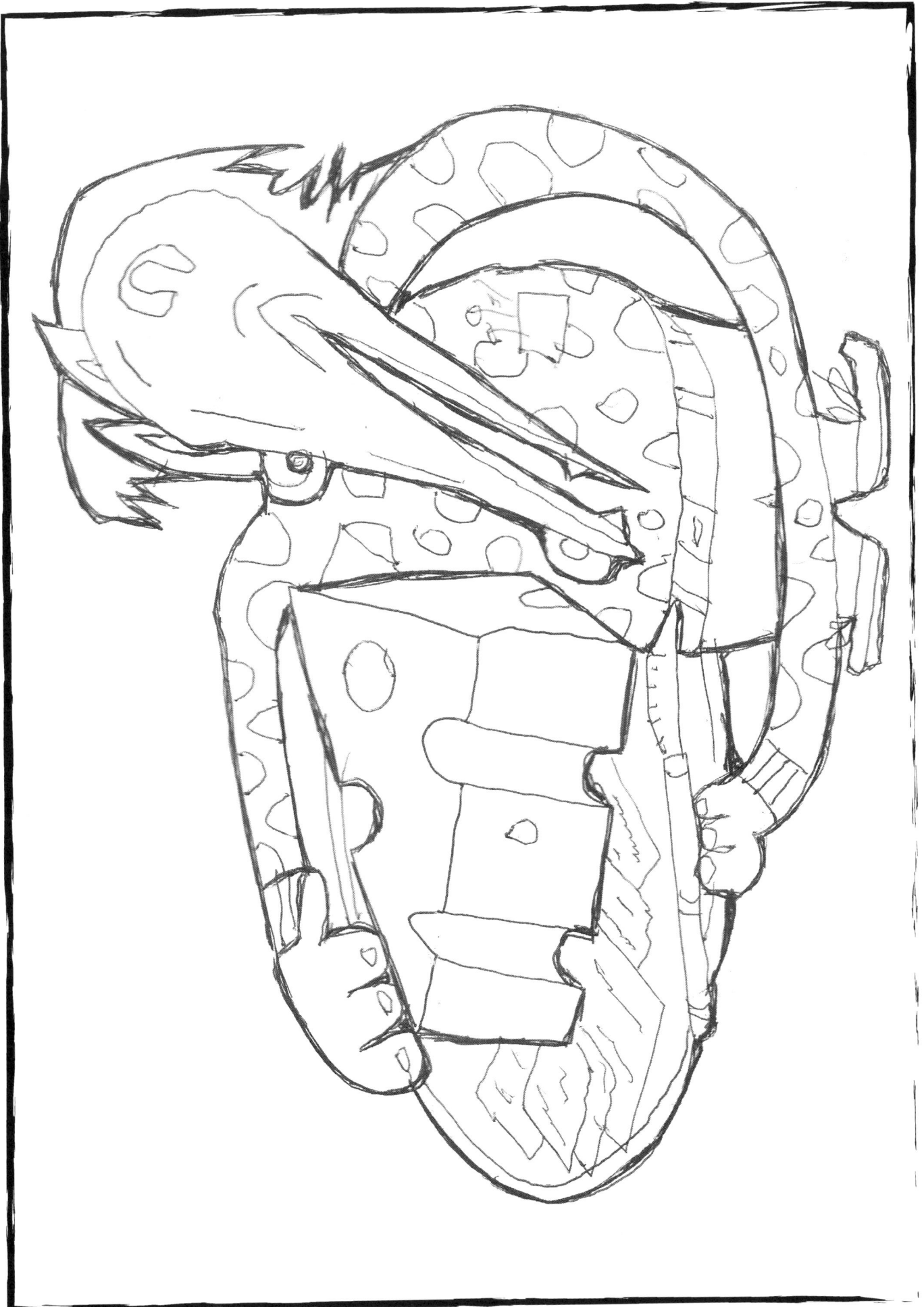

"Pardon me, but do you have any Gruyere-Porcini Pulse Popcorn?"

Hello Everyone. My name is Curly and I am a coloring addict. (Hello Curly)

You can't find this kind of popcorn at the movies. But it is the kind of popcorn you would eat when you go to a drive-in theatre to watch "Far from the Madding Crowd" in your 1934, 2-tone (cream and cherry) Bentley Touring car with the open chauffeur cockpit, and you lean out of your enclosed cabin all decked out in leather and teak woods with silver accessories and crystal glassware… and you knock on the window of the Rolls Royce Silver Phantom discreetly parked adjacent to you and say with a proper British accent, "Pardon me, but do you have any Gruyere-Porcini Pulse Popcorn?"

I never savored the flavor or rode in the '34 Bentley. But my two girls made Gruyere-Porcini Pulse Popcorn one rainy night while watching Masterpiece Theatre's "Downton Abbey" on PBS. They decided to eat something "classy" while watching the British period drama and wanted me to watch it with them. But, as you can guess by now, I was otherwise distracted coloring a swan sheltering her young under her wing in a secluded lake scene. Downton Abbey came and went and so did the popcorn. But you can put on some classy airs if you put on some popcorn and add this simple-to-make recipe. Be sure to keep your pinky up when eating.

Gruyere-Porcini Pulse Popcorn

INGREDIENTS:

FOR TOPPING:
1/2 cup dried porcini mushrooms ground in a spice grinder until powdery.
Butter
Add 2 tablespoons chopped fresh parsley and 1 - 1/2 teaspoons kosher salt; pulse again until powdery.

PREPARATION:

FOR POPCORN:
Heat the oil in a 2 to 3 quart saucepan or pot with a lid set over medium-high heat. Pour in popcorn kernels and sprinkle enough salt to lightly cover the layer of kernels. Remember, you can always add more salt later. Add the butter to the pot and cover with the lid.
As soon as the kernels start to pop, shake the pan back and forth across the burner constantly until the popping slows down. As soon as the pops are about 2 seconds apart, remove from the heat and pour into a serving bowl. Drizzle 6 tablespoons melted butter over 16 cups hot popcorn; toss with the porcini powder and 1 cup finely grated gruyere.

"Rack'em up"

Hello Everyone. My name is Curly and I am a coloring addict. (Hello Curly)

OMG, Rack of lamb is the nectar of the gods. There is nothing that tastes so good (in my opinion, anyway). There is nothing that smells so good. So how is it that I missed savoring this gift to my senses when my family was wallowing in its treasure of pleasure, you ask? That I can answer in one word, "coloring."

Now I know what you're thinking... What kind of doofus sits and colors instead of sitting down with his family and enjoying Rack of Lamb... especially when the smells are driving his senses crazy! Huh? Unfortunately, I can answer that question just as easily. I am a coloring addict and can't help myself. It's a real problem. Once I get into the "zone" of coloring, I'm mellow, and too relaxed to get up from what I'm doing to join my family and get excited about the smells and tastes of what's being eaten or discuss the latest family drama. So it means that I miss out on a few meals, a few details of family life. Oh well, hopefully there'll be some left-overs.

Rack of Lamb with Garlic and Herbs

INGREDIENTS:

FOR LAMB
2 (8-rib) frenched racks of lamb (each rack 1-1/2 lb), trimmed of all but a thin layer of fat
1 1/2 teaspoons salt
3/4 teaspoon black pepper
1 teaspoon vegetable oil

FOR HERB COATING
1/2 head new garlic or 3 large regular garlic cloves, minced
1/4 cup finely chopped fresh flat-leaf parsley
1 tablespoon finely chopped fresh thyme
2 teaspoons finely chopped fresh rosemary
1/2 teaspoon salt
1/2 teaspoon black pepper
1 1/2 tablespoons extra-virgin olive oil
Special equipment: an instant-read thermometer

PREPARATION:

BROWN LAMB:
Heat a dry 12-inch heavy skillet over high heat until hot, at least 2 minutes. Meanwhile, pat lamb dry and rub meat all over with salt and pepper. Add oil to hot skillet, then brown racks, in 2 batches if necessary, on all sides (not ends), about 10 minutes per batch.

Transfer racks to a small (13- by 9-inch) roasting pan.

COAT AND ROAST LAMB:
Put oven rack in middle position and preheat oven to 350°F.

Stir together garlic, herbs, salt, pepper, and oil. Coat meaty parts of lamb with herb mixture, pressing to help adhere. Roast 15 minutes, then cover lamb loosely with foil and roast until thermometer inserted diagonally into center of meat registers 120°F, 5 to 10 minutes more. Let stand, covered, 10 minutes. (Internal temperature will rise to 125 to 130°F for medium-rare while lamb stands.)

Cut each rack into 4 double chops.

"Stack'em high"

Hello Everyone. My name is Curly and I am a coloring addict. (Hello Curly)

My Grandma Irene, on my father's side of the family, introduced me to Potato Pancakes, or "Latkes" as she called them. She was living with my family when I was growing up in Brooklyn and practically ruled the kitchen with an iron mitt. Anyway, she would ask me to help grate the potatoes because she said her fingers had arthritis and she couldn't do it anymore. (this from a woman who "clunked" a Cossack on the head with a candlestick as he rode through her home in Lithuania during a pogrom). I think she just wanted me to do some work around the house and earn my keep. Anyway, the recipe has been handed down to my wife who makes "Latkes" on special occasions, like during the Jewish holiday, Chanukah. You serve them crispy hot and sizzling right from the skillet with sour cream or apple sauce. Just make sure you're not coloring at the time or you'll miss the most delicious treat in the world… like I did. And there are <u>NEVER</u> any left-overs. Oy!

Grandma Irene's Potato Pancakes

INGREDIENTS:

8 YUKON GOLD POTATOES
2 TO 3 TABLESPOONS WHITE WINE VINEGAR
1 CLOVE GARLIC, SMASHED
KOSHER SALT
2 EGGS
EXTRA-VIRGIN OLIVE OIL

READ MORE AT: HTTP://WWW.FOODNETWORK.COM/
RECIPES/ANNE-BURRELL/POTATO-PANCAKES-RECIPE.
HTML?OC=LINKBACK

PREPARATION:

Grate 5 of the potatoes on the largest holes of a box grater. Toss the potatoes with the vinegar and place in a mesh strainer. Place a couple plates on top of the potatoes and weigh the potatoes down to try and squeeze out the excess water. Let sit for at least 30 minutes.

Preheat the oven to 200 degrees F.

Cut the remaining 3 potatoes into 6 pieces each. Place them in a saucepan with the garlic. Cover the potatoes with water by about 1-inch. Season the water generously with salt. Bring to a boil, reduce to a simmer, and simmer until they are fork tender, 10 to 12 minutes. Strain and, while the potatoes are still hot, pass them through a food mill or mash with a potato masher.

Combine the grated potatoes and the mashed potatoes. In a small dish, beat the 2 eggs and add to the potato mixture. Season with salt.

Coat a large saute pan or cast iron pan with olive oil and bring to a medium high heat. Make a 3-inch patty with the potato mixture, cook it, and eat it to make sure that the potato mix is seasoned perfectly. Re-season if needed.

Working in batches, make and cook all the pancakes, until they are brown and crispy and cooked through, 3 to 4 minutes on each side. Blot the pancakes on paper towels and sprinkle with salt. Hold on a sheet tray to keep warm in the oven until serving.

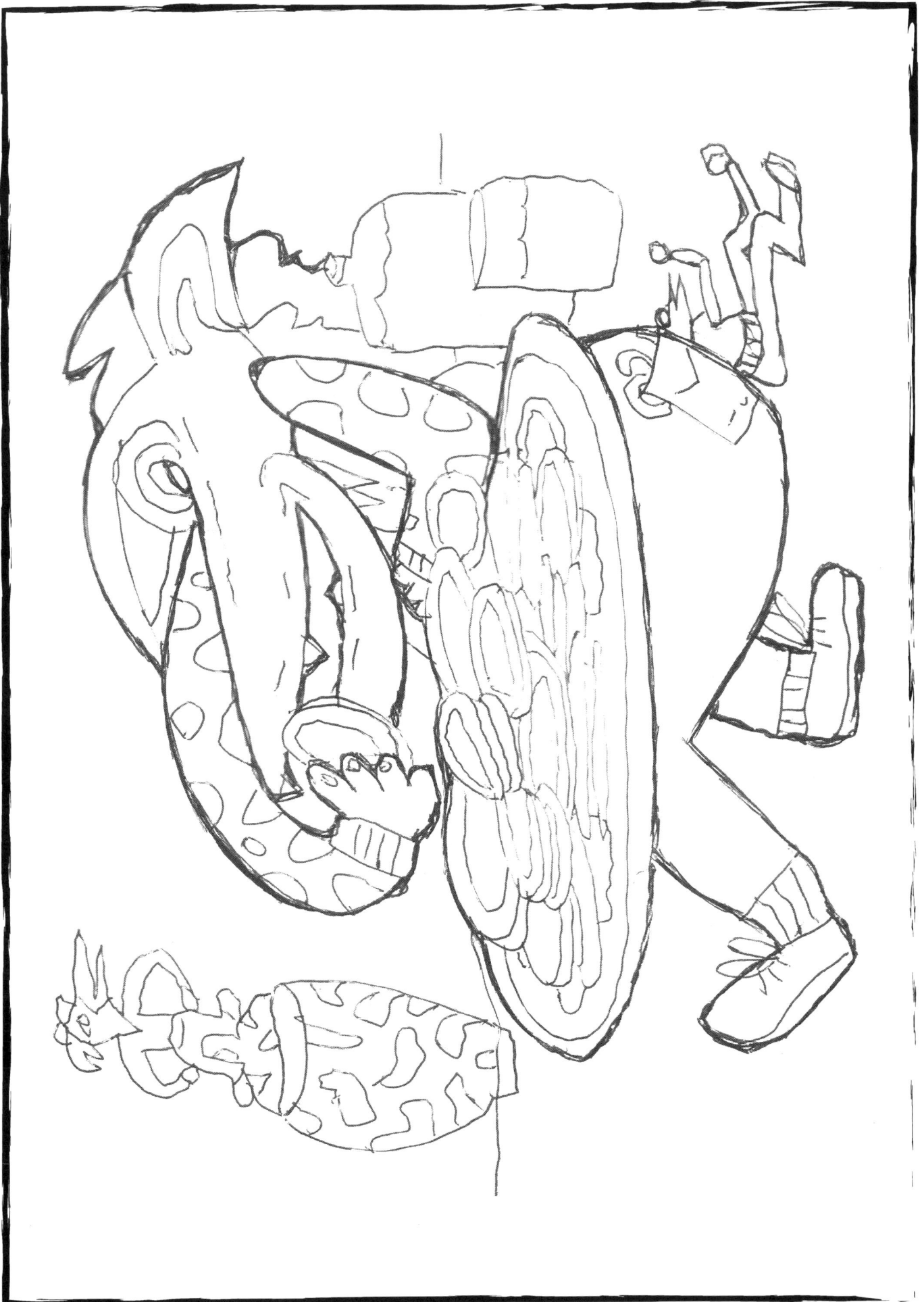

"Au Revoir, French Fries"

Hello Everyone. My name is Curly and I am a coloring addict. (Hello Curly)

There is nothing better than watching a Ravens game on the floor with the kids and the dog howling together in the den on a Sunday afternoon, rooting and hooting after a good play, a bad play or any kind of a play. Nothing beats that… except eating french fries and doing all the aforementioned activities. It's heaven, I tell ya, it's heaven.

Unfortunately, I color when I watch TV, so at around halftime I started this one very intricate doodle and I got interested in that and didn't notice when my wife brought in a platter filled with her "famous" Oven Baked faux French Fried potatoes and plopped them in front of the kids and the dog. Well, faster than a New York Minute those sizzling, crackling and mouth-watering potatoes were gone… inhaled in a nano-second. In fact, by the time I inhaled that wonderful aroma and put down my prismacolor pencils all I could say was, " Hey! Where'd they go?" Much to the amusement of my girls and the dog.

Gilda's Oven Baked "Faux French Fried" Potatoes

INGREDIENTS:

1 LARGE BAKING POTATO
1 TABLESPOON OLIVE OIL

1/2 TEASPOON PAPRIKA
1/2 TEASPOON GARLIC POWDER
1/2 TEASPOON CHILI POWDER
1/2 TEASPOON ONION POWDER

PREPARATION:

Preheat oven to 400 degrees F

Cut potatoes into wedges. Mix olive oil, paprika, garlic powder, chili powder and onion powder together. Coat potatoes with oil/spice mixture and place on a baking sheet.

Bake for 40-45 minutes in preheated oven. Turn potatoes at least once.

"Paella with Pow"

Hello Everyone. My name is Curly and I am a coloring addict. (Hello Curly)

My wife and I were both teachers in the Baltimore school system and both had our summers off. We usually traveled during that two month period. So, one summer BC (before children) we visited Spain, hitch-hiked from one small sea-side village to another and fell in love with Paella. All the seafood was freshly plucked from the ocean and cooked up in minutes (about 35 minutes all told) . So I can attest that this recipe was worth going to Spain for.

We naturally wanted to share this with our friends back in Baltimore and that's when… I won't bore you with the sordid details, but suffice it to say that "coloring" got between me, my friends and a most enjoyable dinner. I don't know how my wife puts up with me. Don't let this happen to you. Hide your crayons where you can't find them when company comes over or when Paella is served. You'll thank me.

Lobster (and/or Shrimp) & Kielbasa Paella (Serves 6)

INGREDIENTS:

¼ CUP OLIVE OIL
1½ CUPS (2 ONIONS) CHOPPED YELLOW ONION
2 RED BELL PEPPERS, SLICED INTO ½-INCH STRIPS
2 TABLESPOONS MINCED GARLIC (4 TO 6 CLOVES)
2 CUPS WHITE BASMATI RICE
5 CUPS CHICKEN STOCK

½ TEASPOON SAFFRON THREADS, CRUSHED
¼ TEASPOON CRUSHED RED PEPPER FLAKES
1 TABLESPOON KOSHER SALT
1 TEASPOON FRESHLY GROUND BLACK PEPPER
1/3 CUP PERNOD

1½ POUNDS COOKED LOBSTER MEAT AND/OR SHRIMP
1 POUND KIELBASA, SLICED ¼- TO ½- INCH THICK
1 (10-OUNCE) FROZEN PEAS PACKAGE
1 TABLESPOON MINCED FRESH FLAT-LEAF PARSLEY
2 LEMONS, CUT INTO WEDGES

PREPARATION:

Preheat the oven to 425 degrees.

In a large ovenproof Dutch oven heat the oil.
Add the onions and cook for 5 minutes over medium-low heat, stirring occasionally. Add the bell peppers and cook over medium heat for 5 more minutes. Lower the heat and add the garlic. Cook for 1 minute longer. Stir in the rice, chicken stock, saffron, red pepper flakes, salt, and pepper and bring to a boil.

Cover the pot and place it in the oven. After 15 minutes, stir the rice gently with a wooden spoon, and return it to the oven to bake uncovered for 10 to 15 more minutes, until the rice is fully cooked.

Transfer the Paella back to the stove top and add the Pernod. Cook the paella over medium heat for 1 minute, until the Pernod is absorbed by the rice. Turn off the heat and add the lobster, kielbasa, and peas and stir gently. Cover the paella, and allow it to steam for 10 minutes. Sprinkle with the parsley, garnish with lemon wedges, and serve hot.

"Just What the Doctor Ordered"

Hello Everyone. My name is Curly and I am a coloring addict. (Hello Curly)

Excuse me. I'm recuperating from a terrible cold and still have a little bit of a sniffle. I was feeling a little fatigued, my throat was a little scratchy, my nose was running like it had somewhere to go and my head was pounding out the Gene Kruppa drum solo from "Sing, Sing, Sing!" So, I went to my doctor of 35 years and told him what was ailing me. Do you believe he wrote out a prescription for Chicken Soup!!! For this he spent 4 years in Med school and 4 more as a resident? I could have told him about the healing powers of Chicken Soup and saved him hundreds of thousands of dollars. So my wife , "Nurse Ratchet", made some Chicken Soup for her poor husband (me) wasting away from double Leprosy and Consumption. So when she brought me this steaming ambrosa and all-purpose elixer, I naturally said, "What, no matzoh balls?"

Chicken Soup with Matzoh Balls

INGREDIENTS:

MATZOH BALLS

1/3 CUP PEANUT OIL
½ CUP MINCED ONIONS
2 EGGS, SEPARATED
1/3 CUP COLD WATER
2 TABLESPOONS CHOPPED PARSLEY
2/3 CUPS MATZOH MEAL
1 TSP. SALT
1/8 TSP. PEPPER

CHICKEN SOUP

1 FOWL, 4-5 LBS.
2 QTS. COLD WATER
1 TBSP. SALT
FRESHLY GROUND PEPPER
1 BAY LEAF (OPTIONAL)
2 WHOLE ONIONS
4 CARROTS, SLICED
5 STALKS CELERY
2 SPRIGS DILL

PREPARATION:

MATZOH BALLS

Heat oil in saucepan; cook onion in oil until tender. Remove from heat. Beat together egg yolks, cold water, salt, and pepper. Gradually beat in oil and onions until blended. Stir in parsley and matzoh meal Beat whites until stiff; gradually fold in matzoh meal mixture. Cover and chill in refridgerator at least 1 hr. Using 2 teaspoons, measure rounded balls of mixture and drop into pot full of boiling water. Cover and cook (boiling) for 25-30 minutes. Can be frozen until used.

CHICKEN SOUP

Clean and cut up chicken. Simmer with remaining ingredients until tender (about 2 hours) Remove chicken and cool soup. Strain soup and skim off fat. Can be frozen. Pull chicken into small bite size pieces and add to soup.

Variation: for a golden chicken soup -- puree carrots in the blender after soup is cooked and add to soup

Matzoh balls recipe by Gerrie Miller, Chicken Soup recipe by Ellie Lapides and Leslie Mehlman.
From Butterfingers Cookbook, Temple Habonim, Barrington , RI

"Could I use my noodle, for once?"

Hello Everyone. My name is Curly and I am a coloring addict. (Hello Curly)

What could I have been thinking? Obviously I wasn't or I wouldn't have missed one of the most delicious meals ever made in 44 years of wedded blintzes. I won't bore you with the details but I was, how can I put this delicately, "lured away from the dining room table" when a beautiful underwater scene needed my attention... fish of every size and shape and color swimming among the coral and flowing sea flowers with shafts of light streaming down through the currents. Well, hope you get the picture, 'cause I did, but lost out on the best seafood recipe of my life. Luckily I found some portions in the freezer on a "fishing" expedition looking for something to eat one day. I fell hook, line and sinker for this meal.

Seafood Lasagna Recipe Yield: 12 servings.

INGREDIENTS:

1 GREEN ONION, FINELY CHOPPED
2 TABLESPOONS CANOLA OIL
2 TABLESPOONS PLUS 1/2 CUP BUTTER, DIVIDED
1/2 CUP CHICKEN BROTH
1 BOTTLE (8 OUNCES) CLAM JUICE
1 POUND BAY SCALLOPS
1 POUND UNCOOKED SMALL SHRIMP, PEELED AND
   DEVEINED
1 PACKAGE (8 OUNCES) IMITATION CRABMEAT,
   CHOPPED
1/4 TEASPOON WHITE PEPPER, DIVIDED
1/2 CUP ALL-PURPOSE FLOUR
1-1/2 CUPS 2% MILK
1/2 TEASPOON SALT
1 CUP HEAVY WHIPPING CREAM
1/2 CUP SHREDDED PARMESAN CHEESE, DIVIDED
9 LASAGNA NOODLES, COOKED AND DRAINED

PREPARATION:

In a large skillet, saute onion in oil and 2 tablespoons butter until tender. Stir in broth and clam juice; bring to a boil. Add scallops, shrimp, crab and 1/8 teaspoon pepper; return to a boil. Reduce heat; simmer, uncovered, for 4-5 minutes or until shrimp turn pink and scallops are firm and opaque, stirring gently. Drain, reserving cooking liquid; set seafood mixture aside.

In a large saucepan, melt the remaining butter; stir in flour until smooth. Combine milk and reserved cooking liquid; gradually add to the saucepan. Add salt and remaining pepper. Bring to a boil; cook and stir for 2 minutes or until thickened.

Remove from the heat; stir in cream and 1/4 cup cheese. Stir 3/4 cup white sauce into the seafood mixture.

Preheat oven to 350°. Spread 1/2 cup white sauce in a greased 13x9-in. baking dish. Top with three noodles; spread with half of the seafood mixture and 1-1/4 cups sauce. Repeat layers. Top with remaining noodles, sauce and cheese.

Bake, uncovered, for 35-40 minutes or until golden brown. Let stand for 15 minutes before cutting.

Originally published as Seafood Lasagna in Taste of Home

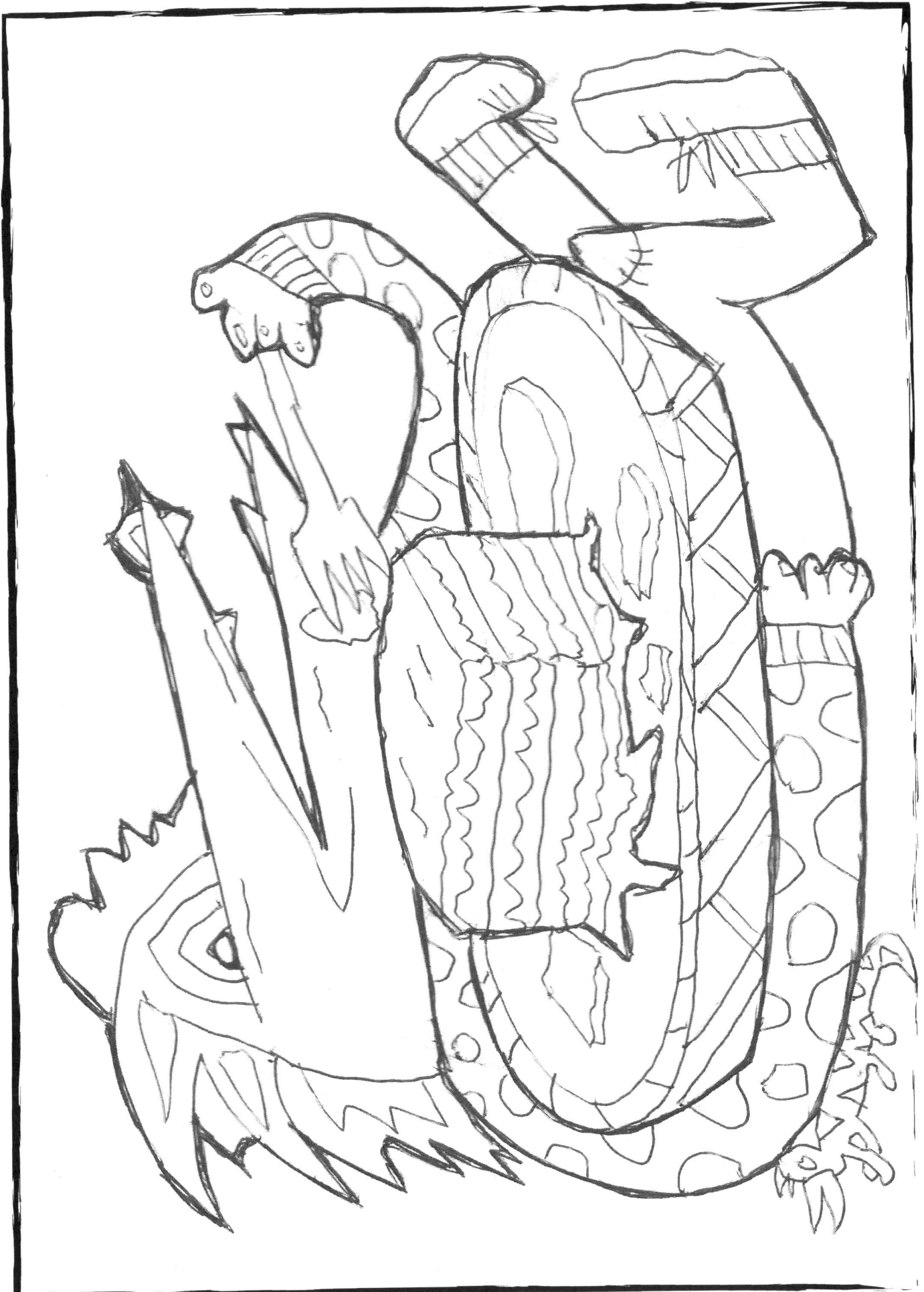

"They called it Maize, I call it amazing!"

Hello Everyone. My name is Curly and I am a coloring addict. (Hello Curly)

When it comes to food, I'm a traditionalist. Once I find a recipe I like, I stick with it forever.
But I have to say, when my family visited my musical daughter down in Austin, Texas and tried her Tex-Mex Corn on the Cob, they said "¡ Ay, caramba !" and immediately started singing its praises in 3 part harmony in Spanish. As for me, I never tasted it. I was otherwise occupied.

Tex-Mex Corn on the Cob Yield: 12 servings.

INGREDIENTS:

12 SMALL EARS FRESH CORN ON THE COB
   (ABOUT 6 INCHES)
3 TABLESPOONS MINCED FRESH CILANTRO
1-1/2 TEASPOONS CHILI POWDER
1-1/2 TEASPOONS GRATED LIME PEEL
3/4 TEASPOON SALT
3/4 TEASPOON GROUND CUMIN
1/4 TEASPOON GARLIC POWDER
REFRIGERATED BUTTER-FLAVORED SPRAY

PREPARATION:

Place corn in a Dutch oven or kettle; cover with water. Bring to a boil. Reduce heat; cover and cook for 3-5 minutes or until tender.

Meanwhile, in a small bowl, combine the cilantro, chili powder, lime peel, salt, cumin and garlic powder. Drain the corn. Spritz with butter-flavored spray; brush or pat seasoning over corn.

Originally published as Tex-Mex Corn on the Cob in Light & Tasty

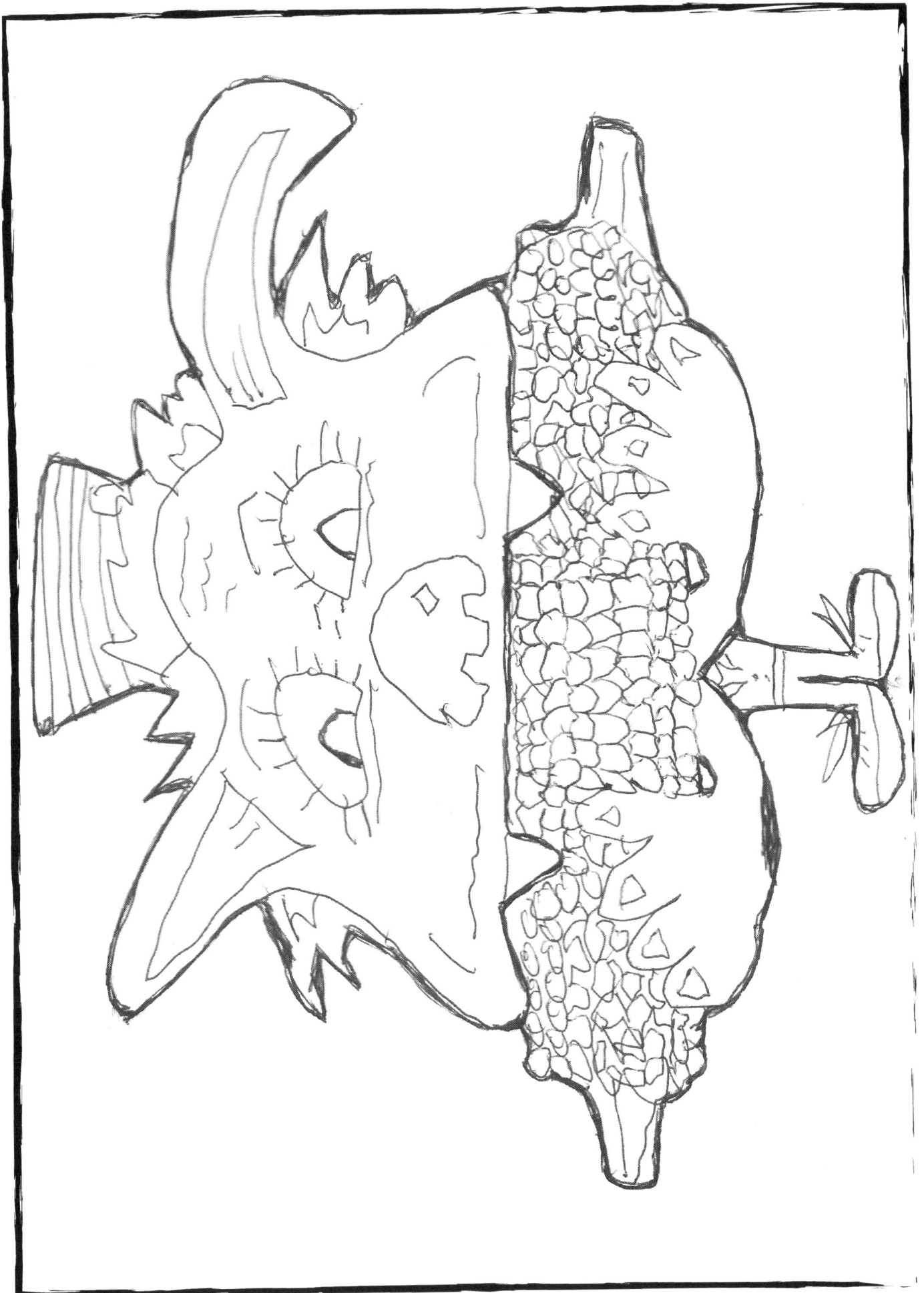

"Mamma Mia, that's a some meata ball!"

Hello Everyone. My name is Curly and I am a coloring addict. (Hello Curly)

Have you every "died and gone to heaven" after taking one bite of something? When I was young(er) and before this coloring craze took over my life I used to visit my grandma Irene, who lived in a small apartment building run by Mamma Rose. Every Sunday, I would "happen" to be visiting my grandma and would "happen" to be passing by the open door to Mamma Rose's apartment. I was standing at the "Gates of Heaven," with the sights and smells of an authentic Italian "dinner" with Mamma Roses's extended family in front of a table with enough food to feed all of Rhode Island. I would "pause" at the door just taking in the smells, when I would hear, "Curly, Curly, come in, manga, manga." I didn't need to be asked twice. "I'm just here visiting grandma," I said to deaf ears as a place was made for me near "uncle Tony" and great-grand daughter Marie. I once asked Grandma if she could ask Mamma Rose for the recipe. So the moral to the story is always visit your grandma on Sundays, 'cause you'll "die and go to heaven."

Momma Rose's meatball sauce and pasta Yields: 10 servings.

INGREDIENTS:

1 lb. chopped beef
1 lb. chopped pork
1 lb. chopped veal, or as a substitute, you can use Italian Sweet Sausage meat,
pulled out of casings and broken up)
2 EGGS, BEATEN
1 ONION, CHOPPED FINELY
3 CLOVES GARLIC, MINCED
1/4 CUP GRATED PECCORINO ROMANO CHEESE
1 STALE ROLL, SOAKED IN WATER AND SQUEEZED DRY
OR 1 CUP ITALIAN BREAD CRUMBS
SALT, PEPPER (1 TSP SALT, ABOUT, AND 1/2 TSP. PEPPER)

BASIC TOMATO SAUCE:

3 LARGE CANS CRUSHED TOMATOES
1 CAN TOMATO PASTE, 6 OZ.
6 CLOVES GARLIC, SLICED
1 CUP RED COOKING WINE (NOT SWEET)
OLIVE OIL
SALT AND PEPPER
SUGAR (1 TSP POSSIBLY)
6 BASIL LEAVES (OR 1/2 TSP. DRIED)
DASH OREGANO

PREPARATION: 30 MEATBALLS

Mix all ingredients for the meatballs at once until completely mixed. Shape into meatballs (use an ice cream scoop to shape). You can either fry them in a nonstick pan (covered when you first put them in and take the cover off when you turn them) or in rectangular pans in the oven, cooked at 400 degrees. Drain the fat off of the pan.

BOLOGNESE (MEAT SAUCE) INSTEAD OF MEATBALLS: YUM!

Brown meats. DRAIN VERY WELL. Put meat in a bowl. Make basic tomato sauce recipe in the pot, add ground meat mixture back into the sauce. Cook for 1/2 hour.

Taste the sauce. If it's too acidic, add a teaspoon of sugar to cut the acid so it doesn't repeat on you.

PASTA: If you don't know how to cook pasta, shame on you.

"Hail to the chef"

Hello Everyone. My name is Curly and I am a coloring addict. (Hello Curly)

Our home was on a Fourth of July Parade route, so it was easy to get caught up in the patriotism of the day by watching the parade. The house would rumble as the trucks, fire engines and bass drums marched on by, and the hundreds of people, led by the mayor of our town waved to all the spectators and potential voters as they watched from the sidewalks, waving their flags. During the summer, there are plenty of locally grown fruits available, so its only "American" to make a patriotic summer dessert to eat while the parade marches by. Just don't ask me to make it, 'cause I'm busy... coloring a flag.

Red, White and Blueberry Fruit Salad Yields: 8 servings.

INGREDIENTS:

1 PINT STRAWBERRIES, HULLED AND
    QUARTERED
1 PINT BLUEBERRIES
1/2 CUP WHITE SUGAR

2 TABLESPOONS LEMON JUICE
4 BANANAS (PEELED)

PREPARATION:

Mix the strawberries and blueberries together in a bowl, sprinkle with sugar and lemon juice, and toss lightly. Refrigerate until cold, at least 30 minutes. About 30 minutes before serving, cut the bananas into 3/4-inch thick slices, and toss with the berries.

NOTE:
Red raspberries can be substituted for the strawberries. The lemon juice acts as a preservative so that the bananas don't turn brown. You can also add watermelon or apple slices and really go a little crazy and throw in... you get the idea.

"Puff the Magic Pancake"

Hello Everyone. My name is Curly and I am a coloring addict. (Hello Curly)

One day I had a craving for pancakes, but not for regular pancakes. Something like pancakes but special, you know? So I went looking through some old cooking magazines and spotted my dream pancake. It looked more like a puffed-up pancake bowl of fruit… holding strawberries, blueberries and rasberries… yuuuuuuuuuuuuuummmmmmmmmmmm !!! and Orange liqueur… double yuuuuummmmm. Now that's what I'm talkin' about. Unfortunately…

Berry-Topped Puff Pancake Recipe Yields: 4 servings.

INGREDIENTS:

2 TABLESPOONS BUTTER
2 LARGE EGGS
1/2 CUP 2% MILK
1/2 CUP ALL-PURPOSE FLOUR
2 TABLESPOONS SUGAR
1/4 TEASPOON SALT
TOPPING:
1/3 CUP SUGAR
1 TABLESPOON CORNSTARCH
1/2 CUP ORANGE JUICE
2 TEASPOONS ORANGE LIQUEUR
1 CUP SLICED FRESH STRAWBERRIES
1 CUP FRESH BLUEBERRIES
1 CUP FRESH RASPBERRIES
CONFECTIONERS' SUGAR, OPTIONAL

PREPARATION:

Place butter in a 9-in. pie plate. Place in a 425° oven for 4-5 minutes or until melted. Meanwhile, in a large bowl, whisk eggs and milk. In another bowl, combine the flour, sugar and salt. Whisk into egg mixture until blended. Pour into prepared pie plate. Bake for 14-16 minutes or until sides are crisp and golden brown.

Meanwhile, in a small saucepan, combine sugar and cornstarch. Gradually stir in orange juice and liqueur. Bring to a boil over medium heat, stirring constantly. Cook and stir 1-2 minutes longer or until thickened. Remove from the heat.
Spoon berries over pancake, and drizzle with sauce. Dust with confectioners' sugar if desired.

Originally published as Berry-Topped Puff Pancake in Simple & Delicious June/July 2011, p17

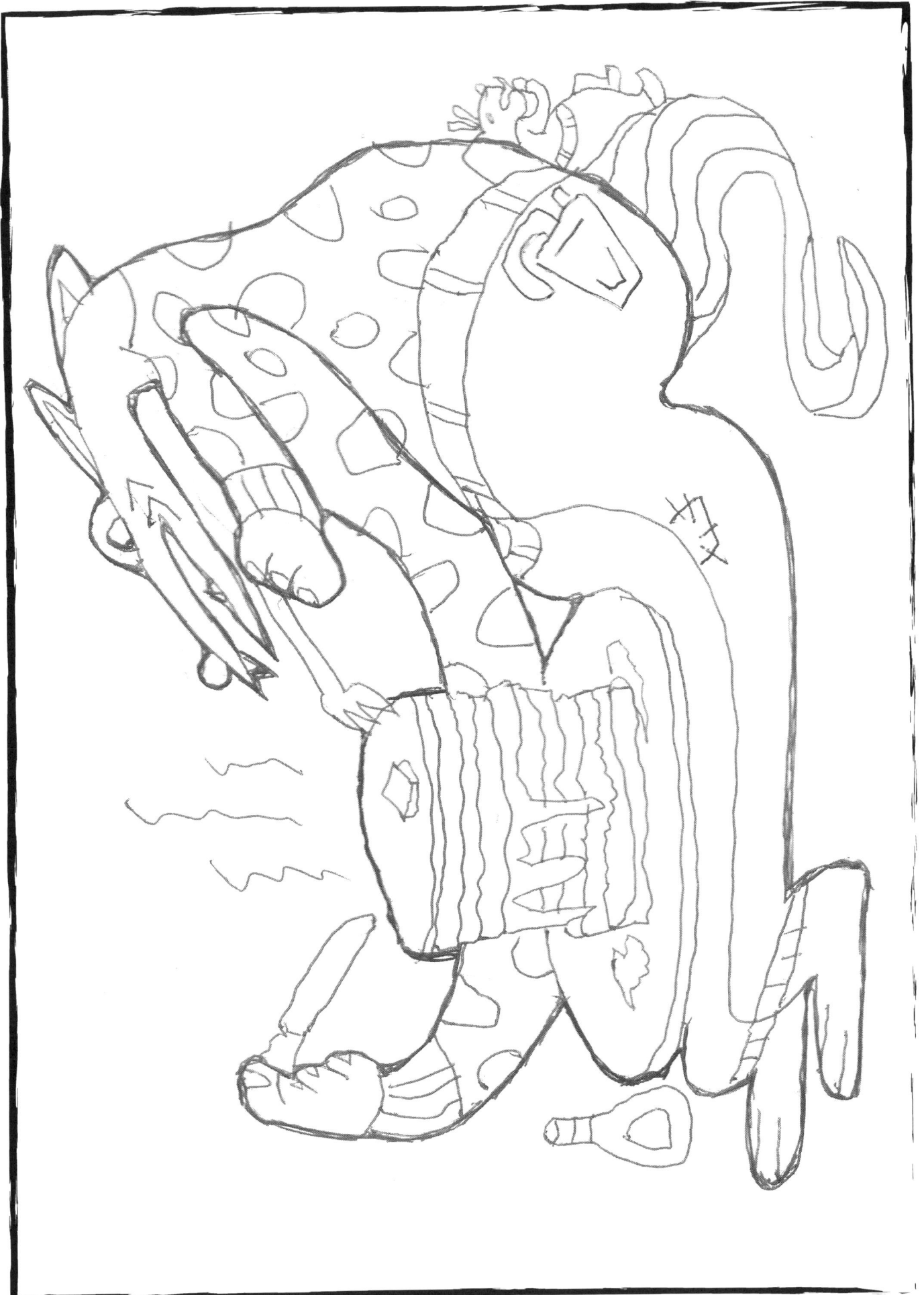

"We all scream for Ice Cream"

Hello Everyone. My name is Curly and I am a coloring addict. (Hello Curly)

That's exactly what happened when I suggested making Sweet Corn Ice Cream to my family. They screamed. They boo'd, they stomped away from the table saying "Dad's gone off the deep end, this time," "I never heard of anything so crazy, Dad!" "Uuuuuuuuuuuugggggghhhhhh! That sounds disgusting." But I knew they'd love it. So I made a deal with them. I would make it and if they didn't absolutely fall head over heals for it I would eat the whole thing in front of them and treat them all to their favorite ice cream. They shrugged in unison and agreed. I followed the directions and whipped up the sweetest smelling ice cream I ever smelled (I even tested the batter to make sure it would satisfy) and went into the den to alert the family that this ice cream was going to throw a party for their mouths. My family went into the kitchen where there were three ice cream cones (waffle) with double scoops of ice cream waiting for them. I, on the otherhand saw a coloring page I was working on and became distracted. There wasn't any sweet corn ice cream left when I finally made it back to the kitchen.

Sweet Corn Ice Cream Yields: About 5 cups, for 10 servings

INGREDIENTS:

1 14 .75-OUNCE CAN CREAM-STYLE CORN
1 1/2 CUPS HALF-AND-HALF
1/2 CUP SOUR CREAM
2/3 CUP SUGAR
1/2 TEASPOON VANILLA EXTRACT
5 LARGE EGG YOLKS
CARAMEL CORN, FOR TOPPING (OPTIONAL)

PREPARATION:

Make the custard: Whisk the corn, half-and-half, sour cream, sugar and vanilla in a medium saucepan and bring to a simmer over medium heat. Lightly beat the egg yolks in a medium bowl. Slowly whisk about 1/4 cup of the warm corn mixture into the beaten egg yolks, then pour into the saucepan and return to medium heat. Cook, stirring constantly with a wooden spoon, until the mixture thickens and coats the spoon, about 5 minutes.

Transfer the hot custard to a blender and pulse until smooth (keep the filler cap slightly open to let steam escape). Strain the custard through a fine-mesh sieve into a large bowl; discard the solids. Stir often until the mixture cools to room temperature. Lightly press plastic wrap directly against the surface of the custard to prevent a skin from forming. Chill until cold, about 3 hours. (For faster chilling, set the bowl of custard in a bowl of ice water and stir until cold.)

Freeze the cold custard in an ice cream maker according to the manufacturer's directions. Transfer to an airtight container and freeze until firm, 2 to 3 hours.

Scoop the ice cream into bowls or cones. Top with caramel corn, if desired.

"It's not only the wiener, its the sauce"

Hello Everyone. My name is Curly and I am a coloring addict. (Hello Curly)

The New York System is a take off of... a Nathan's hot dog? Possibly, but having grown up in Brooklyn about ten minutes from Nathan's in Coney Island, I don't remember a hot dog tasting like this. Be that it may, this is a local gastronomic treat found only in Rhode Island and has reached "cult" status. It is fiercely pronounced by native Rhode Islanders as "The best hot wieners in RI." Who's to argue. Anyway, my daughter lives in Rhode Island and so does my childhood buddy, Mo, so it's only natural that I would "sample" Rhode Island's "finest."   It's not Nathan's, but it is good. So I followed instructions on their website, ordered my wieners from the same place they get them from, ordered their sauce mix and made a passable imitation of a NY System in Baltimore. My family agreed that it was tasty and did remind them of "being in Rhode Island" (what ever that means).

I, unfortunately, was whisked away by the siren call of a "lighthouse on the stormy seas" that I was coloring in the den. But, enjoy and discuss among yourselves the merits of the New York System. Bon Appetito!

Olneyville New York System

INGREDIENTS:

FIRST, PURCHASE THE "ONLY IN RHODE ISLAND" SPICE MIX. IF YOU'RE NOT A NATIVE RHODE ISLANDER AND DON'T SEE THEIR SPICE MIX ON DISPLAY AT YOUR FAVORITE STORE, YOU CAN BUY THEIR HOT WIENER SAUCE SPICE MIX ONLINE AT WWW.ONLYINRHODEISLAND. COM.

THEY USE NATURAL-CASING WIENERS THAT COME IN A LONG 'ROPE' THAT THEY HAVE TO CUT AND THIS PRODUCT IS NOT SOLD IN RETAIL STORES. HOWEVER, IF YOU GO TO THE RHODE ISLAND PROVISION RETAIL STORE ON DAY ST. IN JOHNSTON, RI, YOU CAN PURCHASE THE ACTUAL PRODUCT THAT THEY USE OR HAVE THEM SHIPPED BY GOING TO WWW. LITTLERHODYHOTDOGS.COM. COULDN'T BE SIMPLER.

PREPARATION:

THE INGREDIENTS OF THE SAUCE:

The most important part of this entire process is the ground beef. Make sure you purchase 80% lean (or less) ground beef. If the ground beef is too lean, the sauce will be too dry. Use soybean oil only. . . do not use any substitutions such as other oils or butter.

TO PREPARE THE SAUCE:

Heat soybean oil in a 2 quart saucepan.
Add onion and simmer until brown.
Stir in spice and then crumble beef into mixture.
Simmer, covered, for 1 hour and stir occasionally and mash with a potato masher for finer consistency. If the sauce is too dry after a half hour, add more soybean oil.

Also, when they serve hot wieners, the rolls are steamed. They recommend that just before serving, put your rolls in a microwave for a few seconds and then, before you know it, you'll be lining them up your arm! Really!

"It's time to make the donuts"

Hello Everyone. My name is Curly and I am a coloring addict. (Hello Curly)

When I was growing up in Brooklyn, there was a bakery near the train station called Entemann's. This was before Dunkin Donuts or Kripy Kremes or Tim Horton or whoever your local donut shop is. You can actually buy Entemann's donuts in supermarkets now, but back then there was only the bakery (that I knew of). Anyway, I would be walking to the train to catch the 6:15 am train to Lexington Avenue in Manhattan to go to High School (I didn't go to a local High School, but one that accepted students from all five boroughs who wanted to major in art). I used to get a couple of the most delicious chocolate donuts ever in the whole wide world. Now these donuts weren't just dipped in chocolate on half of the donut, they dripped chocolate all over their heavenly vanilla cake, swimming in velvety chocolate fudge-like icing and every bite was as about nirvana as you could get from New York at 6:15 in the morning. Definately NOT Weight Watchers endorsed. Anyway one day, I was telling my family this story and of course, my children loved the part about eating donuts for breakfast as "we" don't allow that kind of thing in our house. But I thought as a special treat because the Ravens were going to be on in a few hours, We'd make some Entemann's donuts (for old time's sake). Needless to say, by the time the donuts were done …

Entenmann's Chocolate Cake Donuts

INGREDIENTS:

1/2 CUP WHOLE MILK (WARMED)
1 EGGS
1 TSP VANILLA EXTRACT
1/3 CUP COCOA POWDER
1-3/4 CUPS ALL-PURPOSE FLOUR
1/2 TSP BAKING POWDER
1/2 TSP BAKING SODA
1/2 TSP SALT
1/2 CUP SUGAR
2 TBSPS BUTTER
VEGETABLE OIL (FOR GREASING BAKING SHEET AND FRYING)
GLAZE
1/4 CUP DARK CHOCOLATE (PIECES)
1/4 CUP WHITE CHOCOLATE (PIECES)

PREPARATION:

1. In a bowl, blend together the warmed milk, egg and vanilla extract.

2. In a mixer set up with a paddle attachment, mix the cocoa powder, flour, baking soda, baking powder, salt and sugar. Add the butter and blend. Slowly add the milk, egg and vanilla. Mix until the batter is smooth and thick and resembles cookie dough. Leave the dough to rest in the mixer for 20 minutes.

3. Roll the dough onto a floured surface. The dough should be 1/2-inch thick. Using a donut cutter to cut out the donuts.

4. Heat at least 3 inches of vegetable oil in a heavy bottomed pan. The oil should be 360°F.

5. Carefully place the donuts one at a time into the oil. Fry for 2 minutes on each side or until golden brown. Remove with a slotted spoon and drain on a wire rack.

6. To make the glaze, melt each of the chocolates separately over a pan of water. Coat the donuts making a pattern.

Recipe found on the yummly website

"Hey! It's Mohammed Ali!!!!"

Hello Everyone. My name is Curly and I am a coloring addict. (Hello Curly)

As you can tell by now, some of my favorite memories involve food... especially food that I haven't had since back in the day. One such memory took place in the Carnegie Deli in New York with my childhood buddy, Mo. He was having a classic Reuben sandwich and I was having a most delicious Triple Decker Grilled Shrimp BLT with Avocado and Chipotle Mayo. It was AWESOME, believe me. When all of a sudden, who should walk in to the deli but Cassius Clay, the famous boxing champ. I stood up and shouted," Hey! It's Mohammed Ali!!!" He waved to everyone and ducked out, just like that. I couldn't help it, I get excited seeing a celebrity. Years later, I would try to replicate that sandwich, thinking I would take it into the den and color a scene while watching TV. Well, 2 out of 3 ain't bad. You try to eat a triple decker, draw and watch TV!

Triple Decker Grilled Shrimp BLT with Avocado and Chipotle Mayo Yields: 2 servings

INGREDIENTS:

1 CUP MAYONNAISE
1 CHIPOTLE PEPPERS
1 IN ADOBO SAUCE
1/2 LIME (JUICED)
1 PINCH SALT
1 PINCH GROUND BLACK PEPPER
4 SLICES BACON
8 EXTRA LARGE SHRIMP (PEELED, DEVEINED, AND TAILS REMOVED)
1 TBSP OLIVE OIL
SALT AND GROUND BLACK PEPPER (TO TASTE)
1 AVOCADO (PEELED, PITTED AND SLICED)
2 LEAVES ROMAINE LETTUCE
4 SLICES TOMATOES (RIPE RED)
6 SLICES SOURDOUGH BREAD (TOASTED)

PREPARATION:

Combine mayonnaise, chipotle pepper, lime juice, and a pinch of salt and pepper in a bowl. Puree until smooth with a stick blender. Alternately, you can use a food processor to puree the ingredients. Cover and refrigerate until ready to assemble sandwiches.

Place the bacon in a large, deep skillet, and cook over medium-high heat, turning occasionally, until evenly browned, about 10 minutes. Drain the bacon slices on a paper towel-lined plate.

Preheat an outdoor grill for medium-high heat, and lightly oil the grate. Toss the shrimp in a bowl with olive oil and salt and pepper to taste.

Cook shrimp on the preheated grill until they are bright pink on the outside and the meat is no longer transparent in the center, about 3 minutes on each side.

To assemble sandwiches: Spread prepared mayonnaise dressing generously on 1 slice of bread. Arrange half of the shrimp and avocado slices on top. Place another slice of bread over the avocado, and spread another layer of the dressing. Top with a lettuce leaf and 2 slices of tomato followed by a third slice of bread. Repeat with the remaining ingredients for the second sandwich.

"Author's Note"

Hello Everyone. My name is "Mo" and I am <u>not</u> a coloring addict. In fact, there is no such thing as a "coloring addict." There is no 12-step program for "recovering coloring addicts." This has all been a little fun at what has become a world-wide phenomenom. People from all walks of life around the world find comfort in de-stressing by coloring in a coloring book. The very act of coloring relaxes and forces the colorist to concentrate and think only about making something beautiful. It may be addictive, but not in a bad way.

"Coloring generates a balanced calmness and centered demeanor while also stimulating brain areas related to motor skills, the senses and creativity" says psychologist Joanna Futransky, PhD. Lately, in fact, many of her patients have been asking her about the benefits of using adult coloring books to de-stress.

The fact that Curly actually couldn't eat while drawing is absolutely true, but not because he was addicted to coloring. He just didn't want to get his drawings greasy with chicken wings or other food while drawing his doodles. He did have enough willpower and discipline to put his ball-point pen down and join his family at the dinner table. The stories about his "addiction" are fantasy, but the recipes are real. Some were handed down from family members, or friends and others have been found in other cookbooks or the internet.

Curly and I hope you have many relaxing and delicious meals from this coloring recipe book, but don't expect to lose weight if you do. And you should put the crayons down to enjoy life … once in a while.

Made in the USA
Middletown, DE
02 September 2024